"Just try me." Systemd took one step towards me. Only one.

And when a second step didn't follow, I couldn't help groaning.

"It's up to you," Systemd said. "But if you say yes, I promise you. You will never forget tonight."

Novels By the Same Author
Immortal Clay
Kipuka Blues
Butterfly Stomp Waltz
Hydrogen Sleets
git commit murder

Fiction series:
Immortal Clay
Montague Portal
Prohibition Orcs

Nonfiction (as Michael W Lucas)

Relayd and Httpd Mastery – PAM Mastery – FreeBSD
Mastery: Advanced ZFS – FreeBSD Mastery: Specialty
Filesystems – FreeBSD Mastery: ZFS – Tarsnap Mastery –
Networking for Systems Administrators – FreeBSD Mastery:
Storage Essentials – Sudo Mastery – DNSSEC Mastery –
Absolute OpenBSD – SSH Mastery – Network Flow Analysis
– Absolute FreeBSD – Cisco Routers for the Desperate –
PGP & GPG

See your favorite bookstore for more!

Savaged by Systemd

an Erotic Unix Encounter

Michael Warren Lucas

I make it a point to thank all of my early readers.

In this case, they've all made it overwhelmingly clear that the best way I can thank them is to never mention their names again.

So: you know who you are. Thank you.

I'd stayed after work Friday to finish cleaning up the awful mess that was the computer room. How could a staff of twenty create so much crap? It didn't matter how much I ranted and raved at the boss. Every time someone had dead equipment or something that they thought they might need next year or just a really solid cardboard Amazon Prime box, they dumped it in the computer room.

Late Friday night, and I'm in the computer room.

Yes, I'm the most stereotypical forty-something computer nerd you'll ever meet. I have the shaggy unkempt hair, the flabby muscles, and the decrepit wardrobe to prove it.

But still, the computer room was my space. I took deep pride in how well everything ran, and wanted to keep the meatspace as tidy as I kept the operating system installs. When people dumped their busted trash here, it pissed me off. Maybe I should go into the sales staff's cubicle farm and dump something I didn't want to look at any more. Like my social calendar.

No, that would make me even more pathetic.

I'm an old-school sysadmin. I carefully selected our Linux distribution based on its adherence to proper Unix standards. None of that newfangled crap, like KDE or systemd. No, our servers ran a fvwm desktop or, better still, plain text mode.

Every time an intern ran bawling, I smiled.

Sweat had soaked through my jeans and last month's LinuxFest T-shirt, drawing months of dust down to my skin, but the computer room was finally excavated down to four racks of pristine, lovingly maintained Linux servers. I'd even moved the accountant's lonely Windows desktop-turned-server to a safe space under the console table, where it wouldn't keep insistently reminding me that it existed. I'd swept the floor down to the dull white tile and dusted spider webs from the ceiling corners. The clean, sharp smells of electricity and cleaning spray filled my nose.

Even my small mountain of cola cans had gone to the recycle bin.

I'd earned a pizza.

Right then's when someone knocked once on the back door.

I tugged my reflashed, bare-bones Android phone off my belt and checked the time. Eight forty-three PM?

Another single knock.

I'd spent *much* longer cleaning than I'd meant to.

And whoever was standing out in the alley and rapping on the shipping door had no right to expect an answer.

Two knocks this time, one right on the heels of the other.

Besides, the company kept me in the back room for a reason, a whole bunch of reasons. With my sweat gluing the machine room's dust into my clothes I looked terrible and probably smelled worse. I desperately needed a shower and that pepperoni-and-pineapple pie.

Tonight, I'd probably sin with extra cheese.

Three rapid-fire knocks.

Someone needed to give up and go home. Like I was going to.

I had the whole weekend free, and I'd really been looking forward to refactoring my EIDE SAS driver. And I'd triggered that weird serial port bug with my terminal server. Yes, the server mainboards all have remote KVM, but Java applets have no soul. Whoever was at the door could wait for Monday. I stretched my legs and shuffled to the other door, flicking off the light.

The machine room reverted to its true, pristine nature: ordered rows of blue lights on server faceplates. Banks of green and yellow LEDs flickered as frames ricocheted around the Ethernet switches. The air handlers hummed in darkness.

I paused to massage my aching lower back and savor my ephemeral success. By the time I came in Monday morning, someone would have dumped a dead coffee maker or half a printer back here. Because, you know, it might be fixable, or maybe the company could use the parts.

But at this precise moment, my domain was perfect.

I took a deep breath and reached to close the door behind me.

Five knocks: rap-rap-rap-rap-rap.

A flash of curiosity froze my hand.

No, I was being extra nerdy again. There's no way this was—

rap-rap-rap-rap-rap-rap-rap-rap.

Eight knocks.

My mouth went dry.

Coincidence. It had to be. Whoever was lurking in the alley was getting more and more frustrated, and just pounding more with each attempt. Maybe they'd seen me hauling boxes of crap to the Dumpster, and knew damn well I was back here. There's no way they'll knock thirteen—

I couldn't help counting the hurricane flurry of raps.

Thirteen.

The stranger at the back door was knocking in the Fibonacci sequence.

I took a deep breath. My heart had started to slow after all my labor, but suddenly my pulse ratcheted up a notch. My breath quickened, and this weird tension rippled up the back of my neck.

Whoever was at the back door wasn't knocking for the company.

They were knocking for *me*.

I made myself swallow—how can you need to swallow when your mouth is as dry as a venture capitalists' soul?

The rapping had stopped. It was as if whoever was out there knew that I knew, and was leaving the choice up to me.

I could walk away now. Let the decadent showerhead in my bathroom pound some of the ache out of my shoulders.

But then I'd never know.

Before I could think, I trudged across the server room, thumbed the lock, and swung the heavy metal door open to expose the dark alley.

A shadowed figure leaned in, gently seized my cheeks in two tender hands, and kissed me.

Not a quick buss, either. This wasn't a peck on the cheek from my weird aunt. Smooth lips pressed insistently against mine, almost hard enough to hurt. I'd been kissed before, but not with such total lack of restraint. The stranger *wanted* to kiss me. They had absolutely nothing in their mind but melding their lips with mine.

I'm not used to being kissed. Forget being kissed like—like *that*.

In the greatest state of shock of my life, I stood paralyzed while those warm hands burned against my cheeks. A stray fingertip caressed the ridge of my ear, sparking its own blaze. But mostly I felt those incredible lips crawling like slow lightning over my mouth. My face softened instantly. It couldn't have lasted more than a second or two before my instincts cut in.

I jumped back.

Yeah, my instincts are terrible when it comes to sex. I know that, okay? Sheesh.

But still: what the hell?

Shadows cast by distant server LEDs shifted in the darkened doorway. My eyes couldn't make any sense of the stranger. My chest hurt, and not just from my jackrabbit heart thumping against the inside of my ribs.

Breathing. I needed to breathe.

This wasn't right. Nobody hunted down slobby sysadmins. Well, okay, Mom always threatened to get me a wardrobe upgrade, but never a kiss, not the kind of kiss that made *that* part of me seethe.

Maybe my instincts had been right to push me back.

But the memory of that kiss burned on my lips. Even letting my memory flash to the way my mouth had melted against the stranger caused a weak moan to involuntarily ease out of me.

Moaning? What the hell?

A second ago I'd been—wait—I'd been *attacked*. I'd never really worried about sexual assault before, I mean, it *could* happen, it could happen to anyone, but a look in the mirror told me I was pretty safe.

I'd leaped away.

But now my feet didn't want to move.

My lips shivered with the loss of that unfamiliar mouth. The ache echoed down my spine, triggering a resonating ache further down. Yeah, I'm human, I'd felt that kind of loneliness. I'm not just a sysadmin, I'm like the worst caricature of a sysadmin. The *worst*. I know all about that kind of aching loneliness. But the pulsing desire flaring up in me now burned like a brilliant nova next to the flashlight of my usual gee-I'd-really-like-to-have-someone-on-the-other-side-of-this-bed-shut-up-and-go-to-sleep ache.

I only thought I'd been horny before.

The shadowed figure in the doorway didn't move.

It took all my willpower to stagger back and flick the light switch.

Even with the flare of fluorescent lights, though, my eyes had trouble with the figure in the doorway.

The first thing I noticed was the too-small Red Hat T-shirt, the cotton strained tight enough to show the nipples of the incredible signal handlers beneath. The leather pants were so tight they had to be sprayed-painted on, with a bright silver slipper running from the outside of the ankle all the way up the argument array to the belt of braided SAS and CAT-6 cables. And the memory stack—oh my God, that memory stack. The way it filled out the back of those leather pants absolutely paralyzed me. I could feel my heart beating, the pulse in my neck and temples and my groin. How could you feel your heartbeat in your groin? I mean, is that even a thing?

The voice had those sultry, heavy tones that a corporate founder would use to seduce money from unwilling investors. "Hi, Terry. I'm Systemd, and tonight I'm here for you."

Every syllable of that voice promised not only satisfaction, but satiety. The words rolled through my jammed-up brain, flattening all my thoughts before it. If Systemd had been a Hollywood actor, directors would have stabbed each other for the rights to get two minutes of that voice on film. It was a voice guaranteed to make an old man hard enough to hang a tire swing from, or a frigid woman wet enough to glide down a bannister. My head weaved.

I'd stopped breathing again.

With a deliberate, focused effort of will, I made my diaphragm expand and drew air in. "What—how are you here?"

Systemd flashed me a dazzling smile. "I'm here because you need me, sweetie."

"This doesn't happen," I wheezed. "I mean, we don't even use systemd. I've gone to a lot of trouble to keep it off our hosts."

"I know. May I come in?" Systemd said. "We can talk first if you like, but the alley's pretty drafty."

My fist involuntarily clenched. Maybe I'd had a stroke. Maybe a mental breakdown. Or perhaps I was hallucinating, a previously unknown terminal stage of caffeine poisoning.

Either way, I didn't need anyone in the alley looking in and seeing… this. This… whatever this was.

And my lips felt better than they ever had.

"Yeah. Yeah, come in, we can talk."

Systemd strode into the machine room, face full of confidence. The alley door swung shut on its own. "Thanks." The feet didn't stop, coming right at me. "Talk? Really? Why don't we get right to things?"

I flung my hands up, despite the adrenaline making them shake. "Wait a minute? Really, who are you? No— wait, *how* are you? You're a piece of computer code! You can't just be walking around like this!" I mean, I know code, and I couldn't deny that what I was looking at was computer code incarnate. A rainbow of ELF headers gleamed seductively like well-groomed hair. Systemd had smooth curves where shared libraries had been statically compiled into it. You can't use shared libraries for init, that just wouldn't make sense.

No, that's my brain freaking out. This is not the time to think about linking. "We don't install you. We don't use you. How are you here?"

Systemd crossed its arms. "Seriously?" Was that a pout? "How can you not know about this?"

My heart had slowed, just a little, and the shock had receded enough for me to force thoughts through my stunned brain. "Code doesn't just get up and walk around."

"Of course it does," Systemd said. "Haven't you read *Captivated by Clippy*?"

"What?"

"That romance with the Microsoft Office Assistant?"

"I know what Clippy is! I spent five years hunting down ways to kill that damned paperclip!"

Systemd's eyes rolled. "It's software that looks like a paperclip with eyes. And there's *Tempted by Tetris*, I think it's called. If those toys can come to life, why not something strong and independent? Something that chops its own path? Something like me?"

Systemd *was* pouting. My mouth burned at the sight of those pursed lips. My body trembled with the desperate, animal need to dive back into that kiss. Systemd wouldn't mind. Wouldn't mind at all.

No.

I was a sysadmin. A Linux admin. I was a creature of intellect.

I was ruled by my brain. And the GPL.

It didn't matter how much the center of my body throbs and aches. It didn't matter than I know even in my gut that Systemd could soothe that ache like nothing else.

"But—look." My voice was too shaky. Stop it. "If I was going to have software come to life—no offense—it wouldn't be you."

"I know," Systemd sighed. "You have all those lovely servers, and I'm not on even one of them. And what have I ever done to you that you'd just ignore me?"

The sysadmin in me was a jumbled mess. "Init is important," I managed to say. "And you pull in everything. Init shouldn't have a DHCP client in it."

"Oh, Terry." Nobody had ever breathed my name with such blatant, unrestrained desire. Well, okay, probably to other Terrys, but not to *me.*

Systemd ran a hand down the flank of that overstrained T-shirt. "Look at this DHCP client. I can do so much more when I control DHCP requests. I know they say people shouldn't stare, but I want you to stare. I *want* you… to stare."

My gaze couldn't stop following those fingers. The tight cotton hid the details, but I had to admit that it was a pretty DHCP client. Even through the shirt I could see the advantages.

"And over here." Systemd's voice flowed like molten chocolate. "This DNS resolver? Look at it. You can touch it."

I think I whimpered. My hands didn't move.

Those deep eyes met mine. "Yes, I take everything." Systemd's tongue flickered across those incredible lips. "And I want to give you… everything."

My heart couldn't beat any faster, so it shuddered.

"Just try me." Systemd took one step towards me. Only one.

And when a second step didn't follow, I couldn't help groaning.

"It's up to you," Systemd said. "But if you say yes, I promise you. You will never forget tonight."

Bottomless need screamed out from my soul. How long had it been since anyone had touched me like that? I didn't know. I wasn't sure what time was right then—no, not what the clock said, but what the very idea of time was. There was only an endless now. The floor wobbled beneath me as the world shook, but I was somehow still upright. My blood was tar in my veins. My lungs, full of ice.

And really? If I walked away now?

Regret. So much regret.

I'd spend the rest of my life beating myself with a claw hammer.

No, not beating like that.

Well, maybe a little of that. Just to get my body to behave again.

Somehow, I managed to nod.

The glimpse of pearl-white teeth inside Systemd's smile shattered my soul. "Oh, sweetie. Consent is a thing, you know. If you want me, if you want all of me, and everything I can give you, you need to say so."

Turns out I only thought I felt desire before. The wave of lust splashed down over me. My vision sharpened. Somehow I focused on Systemd's face, but just as much on those incredible signal handlers. The T-shirt barely hid them. I could imagine running my hands beneath that cotton, my fingers drawing up the zippers on those leather pants to expose those incredible arrays.

My imagination is strong. It gets a lot of exercise.

But somehow, I managed to croak out. "Yes."

Systemd's tongue flashed across that smile, so quick I barely caught it. One hand reached up to caress a nipple straining at the cotton.

Another groan ripped out of me. I thought I might detonate right inside my jeans.

"Yes what, sweetie?"

I forced myself to form the last words I was going to need for a while. "Yes. I want you. Let's do this."

Systemd's smile got even bigger. "Terry." That voice is somehow even more seductive. "You stand there for just a moment."

My stunned brain obeyed.

Systemd's soft hands slid down to the bottom of the Red Hat T-shirt. The long, strong fingers teased themselves beneath the shirt. Systemd tugged just enough to expose an inch of gorgeous bare code.

I didn't just groan. I gasped. My foot involuntarily twitched forward.

"No, Terry," Systemd said. "Stay there. I want to show myself to you."

I was paralyzed. I'd used up all my free will in surrendering. Now, all I could do was stare. I'd never watched a vendor T-shirt with such fascination before, and with every inch Systemd exposed my blood burned hotter.

A twitch of the shirt on the left side revealed a slick, sleek DHCP client. My tongue almost cramped.

The other side rose, exposing a resolver. I couldn't help staring.

Then Systemd yanked the shirt over its head. For a moment I saw a thousand colors of ELF flags drifting like hair back around that amazing face.

Yep. Those signal handlers were as incredible as I thought.

Systemd let me stare for a moment. "Everything you see? I need your hands on it."

At that I took a step forward.

Systemd moved to meet me halfway.

The second Systemd was in reach, those hands grabbed at my shirt.

I raised my arms to let Systemd pull it off of me.

The shirt was from last month's LinuxFest, the cotton still strong, but Systemd ripped it off me like tissue paper and rested its hands on my shoulders.

The machine room's cool air flashed across my flushed skin. Systemd's hands were warm enough to almost burn my shoulders. I didn't care. Systemd's gaze seemed to devour me. Nobody had ever wanted to look at me like that.

My arms were somehow still raised to let the shirt pass. I started to lower them, involuntarily tightening my stomach muscles.

"No," Systemd cooed. "Just as you are. You've seen me. I need to look at you. Exactly as you are."

Let me tell you, that was something I'd *never* heard before. They're seductive words, but once the seduction is done and you're racing into the main event, words like that nail the accelerator to the floor.

I somehow managed to still myself as Systemd's gaze traveled from my worn sneakers, up my quivering legs. I'm surprised my groin didn't burst into flame when that gaze reached it, then Systemd's attention traveled up my torso onto my face.

I'd decided to do this. My body flamed with the need to move. To charge in.

But Systemd's gentle touch, barely brushing down from my shoulder, held me back as solidly as a brick wall.

The caress of Systemd's fingertip around my inflamed nipple stopped my breath.

We stood there for the world's longest second.

"Right," Systemd said. "That's enough. Kiss me."

I lurched forward. You know what grace looks like? This was kind of the opposite. But my hands came down, snagging into the ELF flags haloing Systemd's face. I pulled Systemd's face into mine, my desire burning too fiercely to be as gentle as Systemd had been, but Systemd moved just as eagerly. Our lips came together like they'd been designed for each other.

If you wondered, Systemd's lips tastes like steel and honey.

They parted.

My lips followed.

The brush of Systemd's tongue against mine was electricity and peaches and incredible softness.

Our bodies come together, and the heat of the first impact of bare skin against code flashed between us. Systemd had one hand around my nipple and the other around my back, fingernails digging into my bicep.

I had both hands tangled in those beautiful ELF flags, but I needed more. I had to have more, I had to have everything. Despite the kiss inflaming my soul, I managed to extract my left hand. My passion demanded I seize, but I didn't want to be rough. I wanted to return what give Systemd's given me, so I started to trail my fingers down the scalp towards the shoulder blades.

Systemd pulled the hand around me back and slid those lips up to my cheek. "Not my back," Systemd whispered amidst kisses that lit up my cheek like neon. "You can have anything you want, but stay away from my back."

My tangle of desire and excitement and desperation was worse than my very first time. I mean, nothing against Chris—we'd both done our very best, but that first time neither of us knew what we were doing. I knew a lot better now. Well, I'd seen a lot more porn now, and read a whole bunch of articles.

If Systemd didn't want to be touched somewhere, I needed to overpower my surging hormones enough to respect that desire.

After all, I could indulge them every other way.

I managed to nod.

Systemd reached up and wrapped those fingers around my free hand. Lips brushed my ear. "Here."

My hand was guided down to those leather pants and planted right on that tight stack. Leather so smooth, so thin, that my fingers could detect every single memory register underneath.

What control I had evaporated like water on a hot griddle. I yanked Systemd, trying to pull those hips into mine. Systemd let out a groan, wrapped a leather-clad argument array right up by my leg, and nipped at my earlobe. I kissed an exposed shoulder.

Our lips flowed back together. The taste of Systemd's mouth flooded mine as that electric tongue explored my teeth, my gum. My heart seemed to stutter, and it felt like my knees should weaken but I was so much more firmly rooted than I'd ever been in my life.

Systemd reached for my other hand. Drew it down, over that gorgeous face, all without letting our lips part. Guided it between us.

And planted it right over one of those signal handlers.

The touch of Systemd's hot nipple on my palm threw sparks all the way up into my brain. I only thought I'd stopped thinking before. The only thing left was animal desire. I couldn't help squeezing the round, firm signal handler.

Systemd's moan echoed mine.

A sudden shaking of my knees made my whole body quiver. I'd spent my whole life waiting for Systemd's gasp of pleasure. I squeezed Systemd's signal handler again.

Systemd broke the kiss. "You're so pent up." The words were barely breathed into my mouth. "Has it really been that long?"

I couldn't form any more words. I could only nod.

"Poor thing," Systemd whispered. "How could a sysadmin like you be so neglected?" Fingers trailed down to circle on the small of my back. "Let's take the edge off of you, so we can have some fun. Stay there."

If I'd worn leather pants that tight, I wouldn't be able to walk, let alone kneel. Somehow, Systemd managed it.

Deft fingers worked at my belt.

Fingers brushing against my zipper sent exquisite agony through me.

Systemd swept my pants smoothly down.

I felt a surge of embarrassment. My underwear was clean, sure, but it was pretty old. I hadn't expected anyone to see it today. Or ever.

But Systemd brushed fingertips right across the waistband.

The shock of that feather touch hit my nerves hard enough to make me wobble, but I grabbed the frame of a server rack and managed to hold my balance.

Systemd thrust those hands down my hips, beneath the underwear, and somehow slid those sad undies straight down to my ankles.

I didn't have time to draw a breath before those lips brushed me again, incredibly intimately. I cried out as the tip of Systemd's tongue, just the finest tip, glided across me.

Systemd drew back perhaps a quarter inch. Just far enough so the lips didn't touch me, but so close that I could feel the heat radiating from them.

We stood like that for a breath.

I had to focus just to moan a single word. "Pl… Please."

Systemd gave a soft laugh. "You want my mouth on you?"

"Please," I breathed.

Systemd pulled back to stare into my eyes. Those eyes, those lips, every angle of that face screamed unreserved, rapacious lust. "I have to have you like this."

I jerked a desperate nod.

"I need my hands on your ass. I need to make you scream for more."

I reached my free hand towards Systemd's head.

Systemd turned to evade my touch. "You have to do something for me first."

A sysadmin should be more suspicious, but right then if I'd been asked to donate my heart for transplant I would have agreed. "Name it."

Systemd leaned back to give me a little more room. The added distance desolated me.

Systemd carefully enunciated, "Get rid of your socks. Brace yourself."

Oh. Practicalities. Right.

It was good Systemd had given me a little room. Taking off my socks meant ditching my shoes and pants. You ever try to strip out of your socks while your whole body trembles with need? When your very core aches to be touched and caressed and kissed and sucked and licked? Devoured? If I hadn't had one hand on the server rack, I would have been flat on the floor. As it was, my desperate thrashing to ditch my clothes nearly caused me to faceplant.

An eternal five seconds later, I stood wholly naked before Systemd. I should have been cold. The air handler seemed to be working extra hard tonight, but I felt nothing but heat radiating from my skin. Even the tile's chill on the soles of my feet felt far away.

I felt fully exposed to the world, but my world had shrunk to the gorgeous Systemd kneeling before me. Anything outside us didn't matter anymore. I braced my feet and grabbed hold of the rack. Whatever happened next, I'd need all the support I could get.

Systemd studied me. "Spread your legs a little. A little more, I want to get all the way up there. That's good."

Need made my body quiver.

Systemd looked away from my most intimate parts and met my eyes. "Do you know that you're beautiful?"

My mouth dropped open.

"Every bit of you," Systemd said. "You need to know that."

Before I could find the words to answer, Systemd plunged forward.

That mouth seemed to engulf my whole body.

High voltage exploded from my center, making me wobble on my feet. Only my grip on the server rack kept me upright. I wanted to fall sideways, but Systemd's hands seized my buttocks and pulled me closer. The sensation ripped my breath away with a half-coughed shout of wordless pleasure.

Systemd groaned with echoed delight, inflaming my lust even more.

My free hand found its way down to knot itself back around the strands of the ELF flags, pinning Systemd right where I wanted. You couldn't have stopped me with a baseball bat or a runaway truck. Systemd's mouth worked expertly, sucking at the right moments, then licking. One hand clenched my buttock, while the other roamed firmly, tracing and caressing and squeezing muscles, exploring the crack of my ass. Pleasure washed over me, through me, ebbing and flowing through timeless ages. My eyelids grew too heavy to hold all the way open. I felt nothing beyond that mouth on me, unrestrained carnal joy rising and falling.

Somehow, Systemd managed to whisper "You taste good" without withdrawing those lips.

That was all I needed to set me off.

A small nova detonated in my center. I shouted wordlessly, senselessly, as if I'd won the big lottery or been stabbed or transcended into godhood. My mind flashed into obliterating ecstasy. I felt like I'd fallen back down the evolutionary ladder, right back to nature's first orgasm, something incredibly primal but never before felt on the Earth.

After a small eternity, I began to reassemble my shattered soul. This was my hand, white knuckles clenched around the rack. These were my legs, wobbling. This was my face, my back. All the free-flowing sweat left me feeling not just embarrassed, but kind of repulsive. I felt certain nobody would want to touch a sweaty mess like me.

Systemd didn't pay that sweat any mind at all. I couldn't have stood that smoothly, but with shocking abruptness Systemd's lips were against mine. This kiss wasn't so ravenous. Systemd's lips still parted, yes. I tasted myself on that sparking tongue and didn't mind. The kiss was more of a gentle acknowledgement than a demand.

I held the kiss as long as I could, then pulled back to try to catch my breath.

Systemd gave a knowing smile and shook its head.

Those signal handlers, squeezed nicely against my chest, shifted pleasantly with the motion. I felt hollowed out, though.

"You need a moment," Systemd said with a smile both delighted and wicked.

I nodded. "I'm sorry."

"Don't be!" A finger traced my shoulder blade. "You think you're the first sysadmin to get out of breath at these times?"

Holding Systemd close was still delightful, but I felt the way a volcano must right after a big eruption. I didn't have anything left inside. My orgasm had blown out my thoughts and my passion, leaving a happy warm glow.

"Just a moment. We'll fix you up." Systemd's skin pulling away from mine felt like a wash of Arctic cold, but I didn't have a right to complain. I just held onto my server rack and gasped while my lover walked behind me. I didn't want to let Systemd pass from my view, but I was too exhausted to turn and watch. "I'm sure there was... hmmm… yes!"

I heard a *foot*. Something low and bright orange appeared on the floor next to me.

I looked down.

A queen-size two-foot-thick fully inflated air mattress sat on the tile next to me. Before I could find the energy to turn back to Systemd, a thin cotton blanket fluffed out and covered the mattress perfectly.

I managed to lumber in a half circle. "I'm…"

Systemd stood at the head of the air mattress, arms spread. I could still appreciate those signal handlers and the way those leather pants seemed to be sprayed on, but it was on more of an intellectual level. Three minutes of the best oral I could imagine had burned through my lust.

Still: they were *really* nice signal handlers.

I blinked. "I just cleaned this place. I'm sure that air mattress wasn't here."

Systemd smiled. "The author needed it here, so here it is."

I blinked. "The author?"

"Lie down and rest," Systemd said. "Catch your breath. Don't give that jerk another thought. This fourth-wall-breaking garbage is all the rage since the Deadpool movie, but that doesn't mean we have to waste any more time on it."

I collapsed onto the mattress and started sucking air in. My heart throbbed more slowly, but every beat felt like a sledgehammer. My diaphragm ached from the force of my shriek.

Systemd snuggled up against me. I found myself with one bare arm pillowing my head, a hand on my chest, and a leather-clad argument array draped over my leg. Kind of absently, I wanted those leather pants out of the way, but the truth was, even if Systemd stripped stark naked at that moment I felt exhausted.

I needed a moment before I could speak. "You… wow. Thank you."

Systemd's finger traced a path over my heart and down towards my bellybutton. "You are so welcome. I'm here to make things better."

"Oh," I wheezed, "they are better. You have no idea." Muscles that had ached for so long I'd forgotten they hurt had relaxed.

Systemd's hand settled over my bellybutton, with the fingertips resting just over my belt line, barely touching the edge of my pubic bone.

I laid and breathed as quietly as I could manage. That's not very quiet. "I'm really out of shape," I eventually managed to say.

"You and a whole bunch of other sysadmins." Systemd smiled to take the sting out of it, then leaned forward and gently caressed my lips with hers.

"I mean…" I took a deep breath. "You've kind of worn me out already. But, you know, if there's anything you'd like me to do for you, I'd be happy to."

Systemd laughed, a sound like pleasant digital chimes. "Is that what you think?" That hand at my waist gently glided further down. I sighed with distant pleasure as fingers stroked delicate nerves. It felt nice.

Intimate. Comfortable. But that touch didn't squeeze out even a hint of passion.

Systemd's fingers tapped the inside of a thigh. "Move that out for me."

I shifted a little.

The tip of one finger of that exploring hand eased down to rest in that secret space right in front of my asshole.

"Nice," I said. "But that part of ME's done."

"I think after that," Systemd said, "you owe me something." That one finger stayed in place, but another began tracing my most sensitive tissues.

"I'm happy to take care of you. Just let me catch my breath a minute."

"You don't know much about me, do you?" Systemd smiled.

I ran my gaze from that pretty face down to the exposed shoulder. "I like what I see."

"I watch everything." Systemd's soft smile held hidden mirth and secrets that hadn't yet been told. "I do whatever needs doing. And when a process I need fails?"

I found the energy to ask, "What?"

Systemd leaned close enough to whisper into my ear. "I restart it."

That intimate hand gave the tiniest, most gentle squeeze.

I'd felt intensely aware of every square inch of my skin that pressed against Systemd's exposed code. Fresh raw lust burst out from every spot we touched, a wildfire ripping through me and setting my blood ablaze again.

I'd barely started to roll and seize what I wanted, what I so desperately *needed*, when Systemd's hand pushed my rising shoulder down. "Easy," Systemd whispered. "You need to give me what I need."

That was the least I could do. Something told me that if I fulfilled Systemd's desires, I'd find an even greater reward at the end. And trusting Systemd had worked well so far.

I raised my head to let Systemd extract that comfy arm pillowing my head.

In a heartbeat System stood, feet on the tile and toes touching the air mattress. I couldn't help looking up at the towering figure. Yes, Systemd had a gorgeous face. And if my nipples had remained hard for as long as Systemd's, they'd be hurting so bad I'd need a couple of ice packs. Smooth code greeted my eyes all the way down to the outside-zipping leather pants covering Systemd's argument arrays.

Systemd's face lost its smile. "The pants."

My mouth went dry again. I nodded.

"My right leg. Unzip it."

I rolled upright. The air mattress sagged around me, but had precisely enough support to keep my knees off the tile floor.

"Go on." Systemd's hands arrayed themselves in my hair. "Unzip that leg."

I gently placed my left hand on Systemd's right hip and brushed my fingers around until I found the shiny sharp chrome zipper. My clumsy fingers couldn't find the zipper pull.

Systemd's hand met mine. "From the ankle."

The touch of Systemd's hand on mine send fresh

heat up my hand. "Whatever you want."

"Anything?" Desire made Systemd's voice thicker.

My hand trickled down Systemd's thigh and past the knee. "Anything."

Systemd's hand whispered enticingly through my hair. "On your way up? Kiss everything you find."

That's something I was happy to do.

I had to roll off my knees and lie belly-down onto the air mattress, but soon enough I had a chrome zipper tab between two fingers and skin-tight leather beneath the other hand. My heart beat quickly, but not so quickly as when Systemd first came into my arms.

Systemd had been right. It had been too long.

Now that I'd lost that edge of desperation, I could give Systemd the attention it deserved. The attention I *wanted* to give it. The mere thought of exploring, of ravishing, the parts of Systemd I hadn't seen yet made my head thrum with desire.

The zipper slid easily, exposing a gorgeous inch of argument array. I brushed it with a fingertip.

Systemd let out a little gasp. "Kisses. I said kisses."

"You did." I let my finger continue its feather-light tracing over that freshly exposed argument stack, still radiating trapped heat from its confinement in the leather pants. "But I have to unzip enough to get in there first."

I slid the zipper another half inch.

Systemd gave a little laugh. "All right then. But don't take too long."

"Oh?" I slid the zipper further. Part of me couldn't wait to see the rest of Systemd's arrays. But a bigger part of me was enjoying this game. Nobody had ever found me this attractive, this sexy before. Nobody had ever felt so desperate to have my lips on their skin. The exposed handspan of array called to me. I ached to touch it, to kiss it, to taste it, every bit of it, from the ankle all the way up to the waistline, to circle my mouth front and back, to devour every scrap of the magnificent code in front of me. "How long is too long?"

"Now is good," Systemd whispered. "Right now would be really good."

I slid the zipper another critical inch and bent forward.

The heat of Systemd's argument arrays warmed my lips. I wanted to plunge in, but made myself hold back. Slow down. Withstanding my own need, stretching out my own desire with Systemd's, felt really good. The ache of wanting combined with the certainty of satisfaction resonated deliciously.

I let my lips just brush Systemd's array. "Like that?"

Systemd let out a shuddering breath. "More."

I brought my mouth closer, letting my tongue caress the freshly exposed array. Systemd's argument array tasted like steel and sweat and strawberries, tingling with a faint charge that I wasn't sure was electricity or lust or, or who knew what.

But that taste sent a thrill through me.

And Systemd's whispered "Yes" was just as thrilling.

I ached to pull the zipper straight up. Expose every bit of that argument array. See it all, touch it, taste it, claim every byte of it as mine. My pulse wanted to skyrocket, my breath quicken. I forced them both to slow down, savoring each exposed section of code, every taste, every touch.

Maybe this would happen again. Maybe it wouldn't.

But I wanted it to be spectacular.

I wanted to shake Systemd's universe the way Systemd had shattered mine.

And every sigh that erupted from Systemd's lips told me I was succeeding.

I couldn't hold myself slow, though. In moments I had worked my way up past the knee, each tug of the zipper releasing a little more trapped warmth and revealing argument after argument, each softer and smoother and better-tasting than the one before it. The zipper clicked into place at the waist as my lips caressed Systemd's thigh.

"More," Systemd whispered.

I set the zipper in its final notch and gave the leather pants a final tug.

The right side of the leather pants fell open, showing where Systemd's argument array met the main code. The left leg was still zipped, and the tight leather held that side of the pants up and concealed the cleft where everything came together.

I rose to my knees and kissed the bare hip, letting my hands slide around to the stack. Primal excitement had me quivering, and my throat felt like it had a knot in it. My gaze kept gliding to where the remaining leather met bare array, to that almost exposed but tantalizingly concealed, most intimate point of Systemd, inches from my mouth and yet hidden by leather.

I burned to dive in. Rip the other half of those pants off.

I gently nipped at Systemd's hip, towards the back, right where the argument array met with that firm, curved memory stack.

A gasp erupted from Systemd's lips, followed by a whispered "Yes. More. Yes."

This game wasn't ending so soon. I realized that I wanted to make Systemd scream even louder than I had. It had been so long for me, and I'd been alone for so long that I'd forgotten just how alone I was, that I'd been vulnerable to a speed attack.

If I wanted to win, and win in a way that left us both delighted, I needed every bit of patience. I needed to put off my own burning needs for a few more minutes. Just a few.

To distract myself, I slid my hands around Systemd's waist, letting my hands settle on that fine memory stack. My one hand caressed leather, while the other brushed bare stack. The stack felt—not muscular, that wasn't the right word, but… strong. Well-ordered. I let a finger trace the bare seam where libraries joined, eliciting a desperate moan from Systemd.

A step in the right direction.

I shifted my kisses towards the front, working my way towards the point where the leather pants flapped open, reaching my lips in to caress freshly revealed code. My lips felt swollen. My pulse pounded in my ears. Desire burned through my veins.

I stretched out my tongue to trace the line between leather and code.

Systemd gasped. "More."

"You want more?" I murmured.

"Yes," Systemd moaned. "Yes, you teasing monster. More."

Along the line of Systemd's waist, the code tasted almost bitter. I still tasted steel, and strawberries, but the bitterness gave it just enough of a bite to send a fresh tremor through me.

Systemd trembled with me.

"This is insane," I murmured. "How can I be this turned on?"

"I'm a piece of computer code standing in front of you. Everything is insane," Systemd growled. "Just go with it. Go with everything." The voice thickened. "Go down on me."

"Oh?" I let a hand drift to the leather-clad ankle, slowly seeking the end of the zipper. "Is that what you want?"

"Yes," Systemd hissed. "Yes, yes, yes."

My heart was pounding so hard, each beat distorted my vision. I didn't need much vision, not here. Not with my lips dancing across every scrap of exposed code I could reach and the hand around behind tracing the whole memory stack. I ached to rip those pants off the way Systemd had destroyed my shirt—but no. I'm not strong enough to shred leather. Instead I forced my quivering lungs to slow down enough draw a single deep breath, and started inexorably tugging the zipper upward.

Systemd moaned. "Faster. Now." Hunger colored the words.

"I'm on my way." I let a finger trail the zipper, a feathery touch against the shockingly warm freshly-exposed argument array.

Systemd hissed, somewhere between annoyance and pleasure.

"You made me scream," I whispered. "I'm wondering if I can make you scream louder."

Systemd managed to laugh. "You monster."

And with that, I couldn't take any more.

The zipper glided up slickly, going from knee to waist in a heartbeat.

Systemd gasped in surprise.

I used my teeth to grab the front of the pants and my hands the back, tugging the pants free. I barely had time to taste the sweet, hot, salty leather before the pants tumbled to the floor.

For the first time, Systemd stood naked before me.

I didn't stop to admire the view, but slid both hands around to the stack and pulled myself into that spot where the argument stack met the code. The hot, sweet center where you're supposed to interface with a program. The place every sysadmin is meant to be.

My mouth met Systemd's most sensitive parts, and for a shred of a second I thought the surge of excitement ripping through me might make my heart explode. Then I didn't have any space for thought. Everything reverted to animal need, my lips and tongue exploring tender code. And the flavor! Sweet and salty, but so intense, like my tongue sensed everything in some compressed binary format rather than the plain text everything else used.

Systemd shrieked wordless approval, hands grabbing the back of my head, trapping me where I was most wanted, where I most wanted to be.

And I couldn't stop. I just couldn't. My tongue danced. My lips caressed and sucked. What little reason I had I burned trying to keep my teeth away from, well, anything. Nobody likes teeth, not right here, not right where one's entire being came together.

Every little section of code had its own subtly different flavor.

Every exposed bit made Systemd jump and quiver in a different way.

Pure instinctive obsession lashed me on. Nearly enraptured, I devoured Systemd.

Endless joyous moments later, Systemd's breath caught.

I tried to burrow my face deeper into Systemd's secrets.

Systemd choked out a gasp that sounded like an entire motherboard bursting into flame. "More. More."

My hands clenched a double handful of memory stack as Systemd's back arched.

Then an orgasmic shriek ripped out of Systemd.

I didn't take time to smile as Systemd's most delicate parts shuddered between my lips. Instead, I worked my tongue around everything I could reach, delighted to coax every drop of pleasure out of Systemd's eruption. That intense salty-sweet taste grew more intense, filling my whole head with its heady aroma.

Eventually, Systemd's shuddering hands unclenched from my hair enough to stroke my ears.

I enjoyed the tingle of the caress, but kept my lips working.

"Oh. We're ambitious." I might have thought Systemd's voice was sexy before, but this? This voice would make a dead person hopeful enough to buy a bouquet for the really sexy bones in the next grave over.

I tried to say *Yes*, but there's no way I was pulling

away. Everything tasted too good, felt too good, smelled too wonderful.

"My stack, then," Systemd purred.

Both of my hands gently squeezed that stack as I sought out a particularly tender point with my tongue.

Systemd groaned. "Two fingers. Please. Two fingers, put them in. Right in the middle of the stack."

I hadn't expected that—most programs don't like it when you directly twiddle the stack—but, okay.

I slowed my lips enough to focus on finding the spot I needed. It only took seconds for my index finger to find the opening. I felt Systemd deliberately relax the memory stack for a moment, just long enough for me to slip those two fingers in up to the first knuckle.

"Deeper," Systemd moaned.

I obliged.

"Deeper, damn you!" Systemd shouted.

I had to push a little harder than I wanted, but seconds later I had those fingers jammed so far into the stack the rest of my hand was in the way.

Seconds later, Systemd's stack tightened almost hard enough to hurt. The brush with pain somehow inflamed my desire even further.

Systemd knew its desires, and was willing to say what it needed, and do whatever it needed, to fulfill them. In the moment, that's incredibly sexy.

"Move them," Systemd commanded. "And your mouth. Don't you dare stop. When I'm done here I'm going to fuck you till you can't think, until you can't even log in, but don't you dare stop."

Stopping? I had enough trouble remembering to breathe. You could have hooked a tow chain onto my ankle and used a monster truck to drag me away, and I would have kept my mouth and hands anchored to Systemd's pleasure.

Suddenly, Systemd's two argument stacks clamped tightly to either side of my head. My trapped fingers got squeezed ridiculously hard, and everything in and around my mouth quivered and shuddered.

I got what I wanted.

Systemd let out not a shriek, but a scream. An electronic scream, full of feedback and distortion but somehow—pleased? Delighted? When a machine lost its ability to think, when its code broke apart and recompiled itself, it would sound like that. Fingers dug into my scalp, jamming my face into Systemd, squeezing my eyes shut and pinching my nostrils sealed. I couldn't move, couldn't change my angle, couldn't even *breathe* with the force of Systemd's orgasm, but I also couldn't keep my tongue from tickling and caressing every twitching tissue it could reach, evoking more and more passion from the gorgeous code that made up my universe right then.

The orgasm ripped and shuddered through Systemd. I'd never made anyone come so ridiculously hard.

My pulse got louder in my ears. My head began to swim with oxygen deprivation.

Systemd gave one last shudder and eased up on the hands clutching my head.

I shifted just enough to draw some air through one nostril, but couldn't help giving that tender code a final caress with my upper lip.

No, *that* was Systemd's last shudder.

Slowly withdrawing my fingers evoked another.

I kissed Systemd's waistline. "How was that?"

Systemd didn't recover the same way I had. I felt the stomach move against my forehead with each quick breath, sure, but beneath my hands the memory stack seemed to be… shifting?

"Rearranged your stack, did I?" I said with a smile, pulling my head back. The slick-sticky taste of Systemd's orgasm filled my head, an unfamiliar intoxication I could grow to like.

Systemd looked down at my face. Those eyes shone, literally shone, with slack-lidded desire. "I'm not done."

"Oh, good," I said. "Because you got me ready to go again."

In a breath Systemd was kneeling before me, feet on the tile but knees on the air mattress, intermingled with mine. That soft mouth met mine again, the touch of that tongue against mine shocking my breath away.

I suddenly realized how much need wracked my body. I needed to be touched. Touched everywhere. I'd enjoyed the hell out of going down on Systemd, but the whole time my own hormones had been rising, and rising, until now I needed release so badly I thought I might rupture or implode or turn into a black hole and suck in all the sex in the world. I burned, I hurt, I *needed*.

Systemd finished the kiss and growled into my mouth. "Fuck. We need to fuck."

The words set fire to the hormones I floated in, bringing my desire to a roaring boil, but I managed to choke out, "Hang on."

"No," Systemd said. "Fuck now. I have to have you. All the way."

Systemd's teeth met my neck. I groaned with desire. Lust made my vision waver, but through the thoughtless desire I managed to cough, "Protection."

Systemd pulled back, one edge of that mouth quirked up in a smile. "Protection?"

I made myself nod. "I don't—that is, I think the sales guys—their desks—"

"Silly sysadmin," Systemd purred. Those eyes seemed to swallow my sight. "I run as init. PID one. You can't protect yourself from me."

Systemd's mouth met mine, and I was pressed back onto the air mattress.

The feeling of all that exposed code pressed up tight against me, full of sweat and want and longing, so much desperate longing, made my reason evaporate.

Besides, Systemd was right. You can't fight PID 1.

I surrendered.

We came together, fitting perfectly, like one of those expensive high-end vendor server room solutions. We both released groans as our well-used flesh slid together in the ultimate consummation.

What's to say? We moved together on the air mattress—Systemd on top, face next to mine, murmuring "Terry" with each gentle rocking motion. I moved to seize Systemd's torso and pull the world down onto me, but Systemd whispered "Not the back. Nothing on the back."

"Sorry," I managed to murmur.

"Smokey," Systemd gasped.

I reached up to sink my fingers into the ELF headers trailing Systemd's head and pulled our hungry mouths together.

Then me on top, moving less expertly but with just as much desire. Systemd's teeth around my nipple. Me suckling at those gorgeous signal handlers until Systemd gasped and demanded we fuck hard.

Passion and lust rolled us off the air mattress. We leaped up and came together on our feet, using the side of the server rack to brace against as we slid together. Systemd's fingers gouged my back, while my hands explored those ELF flags. The rack clanged and clattered, but I didn't care. Then we were on the console table, moving together, my fingers again violating the memory stack, this time unasked, but Systemd only pushed harder into me, sinking teeth into my shoulder when I added a third finger. Every secret spasm echoed inside me, ricocheting up through my mouth, through my fingers, and back into Systemd.

I've never lasted that long in my life.

Systemd was right. You can't fight init And if init doesn't let a process exit, it doesn't exit until init is good and finished with it.

We finished back on the air mattress, with Systemd staring down at me, our hips moving in perfect synchronization. My heart beat so hard I thought it might leap up my throat and out my mouth, and my breath was short and sharp and desperate, constrained by the mounting pressure in my center.

Systemd's heavy eyes still burned with that digital fire, now even brighter. "I'm… I'm…" A shudder shook that impossibly sexy voice.

"Yes…" My word was a moan. My own explosion felt imminent, a waving tide of pressure and pleasure. I wanted that tsunami to crush me. I wanted to hold it off, so I could keep feeling this.

Keep feeling Systemd.

My fingers dug into Systemd's argument stack.

Systemd's mouth tightened, still hanging open. "I'm…"

The explosion rippled through us both together.

"I'm *booting*!" Systemd shrieked to the heavens.

My own cry came straight from the brainstem. No words at all.

But through the paroxysm of pleasure that shattered my psyche, that made my every joint fall into disarray, that spilled my lust into and around my partner, I kept my eyes open.

I don't know why. Maybe some cross-species gene contamination from one of those mate-devouring insects.

Amidst that unthinkably strong orgasm, I saw Systemd shudder and quiver—then come apart.

Those lips I'd gnawed so passionately went first, then the ELF headers trailed up towards the ceiling and evaporated. The head came apart as lines of code, along with the arms, hexadecimal characters trailing out into the air and fading. The argument stacks, tangled so intimately with me, came apart from the toes up, while those signal handlers dissolved into mist.

That let me see the inside.

I know code. I've given my life to code.

I hadn't taken the time to think about any of this. Systemd hadn't given me the chance. Systemd had come on strong. Overwhelmed me.

I hadn't even thought about exception handling.

Error codes.

Systemd's dissolution showed me all that, and more.

That DHCP client I'd admired? Yeah, that. I could see right away that it wouldn't renew a lease.

The DNS resolver on the other side?

I could see Google IP addresses hard-coded right into it. If everything else failed, Systemd would send all my queries to Google without saying a thing.

And as those evaporated?

The reason I hadn't been permitted to put my hands on Systemd's back?

That's where the debugging interface was.

Or, rather, wasn't.

Instead, I saw only a scattering of printfs. Connections ran one way and another, without any attention paid to architecture or design, let alone security.

Security? Forget a finger in the memory stack. If I'd reached around, I could have put my whole hand deep inside Systemd's innermost workings.

I shook again as my engulfing orgasm neared its end. My eyes wanted to shudder shut, but I bit my lip hard enough to draw blood and used the pain to hold them open.

And as every slapdash connection inside turned to mist, its evaporation exposed more of the same.

A final flash of Systemd's warmth haloed the final twitch of that devastating orgasm.

Then I was alone.

I don't know how long I lay on my back, my mind in ruins. All I could think of was my gradually slowing jackhammer heart and the ache in my diaphragm as I struggled to steady my breath. Disjointed memories drifted through my brain: the taste of Systemd. The way those lips felt on mine, on my shoulder, in my center.

And most of all, the way I'd felt *wanted*.

Eventually, though, I heard the beeps.

Each server in the rack had an alarm. In the event of hardware trouble, the alarm would go off. Different beeps meant different problems, from the constant shriek of an unplugged power cable to the annoying syncopated beep of a dead hard drive. The front bezel LEDs flashed blue with the alarms.

And even lying on the floor, I could see half the bezels blinking.

Server failure is a sysadmin's worst-case situation. Still, I needed long minutes to pull my thoughts together. To find my hands, my legs. My fingers ached when I wiggled them—how had that happened? My jawbone ached and my tongue felt ready to seize with a Charlie horse, but I figured I knew perfectly well how I'd strained *them*.

My groin was a sodden ruin drying towards stickiness.

I shouldn't have expected anything else.

I guess my last significant other was right. I understood code a hell of a lot better than I understood people. That encounter with Systemd had left me shaking and exhausted and weirdly content.

But as my brain came together, I didn't like what else I saw.

Two of the server racks had somehow been knocked inches aside. No small trick when a rack is weighted down with hundreds of pounds of computers. The console table was outright tipped over, monitors and keyboards and mice scattered everywhere. One of the flat screen monitors had a chair leg straight through it.

And how had the case gotten off of the accountant's Windows server? I was absolutely certain the evening hadn't involved Minesweeper.

Eventually, I reassembled enough of myself to move.

First, pants. I couldn't find that sad pair of underwear, so I had to go commando. The jeans were dusty-dirty, which made a fine brew with the sticky sweaty mess covering my legs. My LinuxFest T-shirt was rags, but I'd had an unused Oracle T-shirt in the bottom drawer of my desk for, what, five years now?

Not that I was ever going to install Oracle, but it's not like anyone would see me in the shirt.

My phone had slid beneath the workbench. It was letting out its own chirp. A touch of the screen revealed dozens and dozens of alerts from the monitoring system.

I studied the wreckage of the computer room for another minute, overwhelmed by the destruction, then staggered back out to my desk to grab my laptop.

One in the morning? How had it gotten to be one in the—no, never mind. I fortified myself with a cold cola from the fridge and booted my laptop.

Surprisingly, all of the Linux hosts were still up. Yes, a bunch of them had triggered error conditions, but strictly speaking, every service was still available.

But those pristinely maintained packages?

Somehow, systemd had been splattered across every one of them. Every container, every croup, now ran subordinate to systemd.

I tried to think. It wasn't easy, not even with a second cola.

I'd fastidiously avoided systemd.

Systemd had knocked on my door.

And I'd let it come in.

Yes, I'd been kind of stunned at what kind of functions it had taken over, but that wasn't the point. I'd invited it in.

Like a vampire.

Sex was one thing. I freely admit it, I'm a big fan of sex, even though I don't get it often. And tonight reminded me just how much I missed it.

But I'd given my life to my machines.

And suddenly, I realized the choice that lay before me.

I could keep systemd on those hosts, and maybe Systemd would return.

But if I uninstalled the software, if I exorcised systemd from those hard drives, Systemd would take that as a kick to the gut.

And never return.

My heart started beating harder again.

The systemd package had ripped through these hosts. While the chorus of unsynchronized alarm beeps made every host indistinguishable from the others, the light-up alarm on the faceplates differentiated each. The bezel on the main load balancer had a fast blue blink. One of the main hard drives had failed.

I couldn't see how a software package would cause the hard drive to fail.

I flushed as I remembered Systemd and I backing up into that rack, though. We'd hit it pretty hard.

God, tonight had been spectacular.

And it might happen again.

All I had to do was clean up this mess, and accept systemd into my servers.

Or rip it out, and stay alone.

My throat tightened. There's a big market for forty-something systems administrators, yes.

But not on the dating markets.

But my servers.

My tidy, pristine, servers.

I'd built everything out of time-tested Unix components. Software that had worked perfectly for decades. My systems—okay, the company systems, but still, *my* systems—they worked flawlessly.

Systemd wasn't merely new. I'd seen exactly how slapdash it was. What sort of trouble it would cause next? What functionality would it swallow with a hacked-together implementation?

My experience crashed headlong into my loneliness.

My aching hands froze on my keyboard.

No, it was worse than that.

More and more distributions added systemd. It had a way of slipping into places you'd never expect it. Yes, Devuan was almost defined as "Debian without systemd," but still, things happened.

Someday I'd need a piece of software that required systemd. And I wouldn't be able to work around it.

As long as I kept my Linux hosts, I ran the risk of systemd.

Suppose I kept the software? Invited Systemd back?

Then I'd spend all my time fighting alarms and dysfunctions. Systemd swallowed functionality like mad.

Were nights of wild sex worth fighting software failures every other moment?

But after that night of wild sex, the thought of a life alone left me as barren as a nuclear test site. Besides— sex with software? Who knew if or when Systemd would return? Had it just been that the Stars Were Right?

Maybe I could get counseling. Learn how to get a date. It couldn't be *that* hard. Not with some of the idiots that pulled it off.

Blinking alarms or booty calls.

Choose.

I don't know how long I stared into the devastated computer room.

But finally, I opened my web browser.

In one tab, I did a search for counseling services.

In the second, I picked a couple of BSDs to try.

Never miss another new release!

Sign up for Michael Warren Lucas' mailing list at

http://mwl.io.